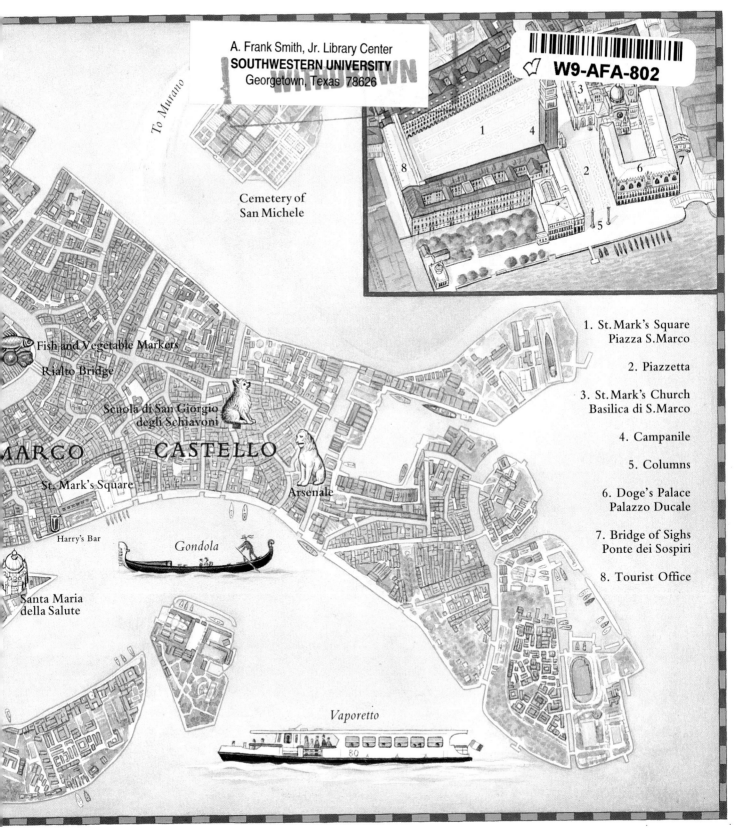

To Murano

Cemetery of
San Michele

Fish and Vegetable Markets

Rialto Bridge

Scuola di San Giorgio
degli Schiavoni

MARCO

CASTELLO

St. Mark's Square

Arsenale

Harry's Bar

Gondola

Santa Maria
della Salute

Vaporetto

80

1. St. Mark's Square
   Piazza S. Marco

2. Piazzetta

3. St. Mark's Church
   Basilica di S. Marco

4. Campanile

5. Columns

6. Doge's Palace
   Palazzo Ducale

7. Bridge of Sighs
   Ponte dei Sospiri

8. Tourist Office

Rabén & Sjögren Stockholm
raben-sjogren@raben.se
http://www.raben.se

Translation copyright © 1999 by Patricia Crampton
Originally published in Sweden by Rabén & Sjögren under the title *Vendela i Venedig*
Text copyright © 1999 by Christina Björk
Illustrations copyright © 1999 by Inga-Karin Eriksson
Designed by Inga-Karin Eriksson and Christina Björk
Printed in Italy
First American edition, 1999

Photographs copyright © Nisse Peterson (pages 12, 42, 55, 58–59, 87 i.a.),
Osvaldo Böhm (page 26), Edizioni Filippi (pages 78, 79), Magnus Lindblom (page 91)
Remaining photographs copyright © Christina Björk/Inga-Karin Eriksson/Göran Österlund
Paintings copyright © Accademia Museum/Osvaldo Böhm (pages 60–62),
Scuola di San Giorgio degli Schiavoni/Osvaldo Böhm (pages 72–75)

The book is set in Bembo 13/16,
a typeface drawn directly from Aldus Manutius's typeface.
Manutius was Venice's most famous publisher and printer of books.
He was probably born in 1450 and died in 1515.
He also created the world's first italic typeface.
Typeface cut by Francesco Griffo

Library of Congress Cataloging-in-Publication Data
Björk, Christina, 1938–
    [Vendela i Venedig. Swedish]
    Vendela in Venice/Christina Björk; pictures by Inga-Karin Eriksson;
translated by Patricia Crampton. -- 1 st ed.
    p.   cm.
Summary: On a visit to Venice with her father, Vendela experiences
the richness and beauty of the city and its palaces, gondolas, and statues.
    ISBN 91 29 64559 X
[1. Venice (Italy)--Fiction.] I. Eriksson, Inga-Karin, ill.
II. Crampton, Patricia. III. Title.
PZ7.B52857Ven 1999
[Fic]--dc21   98-49243
                                                             CIP

Vendela in VENICE

Christina Björk
Pictures by Inga-Karin Eriksson
Translated by Patricia Crampton

R&S
BOOKS

Stockholm   New York   London   Adelaide   Toronto

Contents

Foreword

Every child should have a chance to visit Venice, because it's like a fairy-tale city. Inga-Karin and I know that; we were lucky enough to go there when we were more child than adult. I was fourteen when I went to Venice with Uncle Ragnar, Aunt Alice, and my cousin Jan.

When I traveled with my father, he had always done his advance reading and we absolutely had to go to all the churches. It was the same with his brother. Uncle Ragnar steered us around to the various sights and explained how wonderful it all was. He talked about the four bronze horses on the gallery over the main entrance of St. Mark's Church, so that they almost came alive for me. How the horses were carried off in different wars and are so old that no one really knows *how* old. And yet they are so remarkably beautiful.

From the letters I wrote home, I gather that the many paintings in the Accademia Museum were not as much fun, but the food was great: spaghetti and pizza, the latter then (1953) quite unknown in Sweden.

I have never forgotten that trip. And I still wear around my neck the little silver winged lion of St. Mark which I bought with the money I had saved.

Inga-Karin and her brother Torbjörn on the Rialto Bridge

• Inga-Karin went to Venice with her mother and brother when she was sixteen. It was only a day trip, but Venice was a dramatic and extraordinary experience, all the same. There was a storm that day, and water splashed over from the canals and in through the doors of buildings. It felt as if the town really was

Christina, Uncle Ragnar, Aunt Alice, and Cousin Jan in St. Mark's Square and the little silver lion of St. Mark

threatened by all the water. Back home, Inga-Karin's mother wrote an article about Venice for the local newspaper, and Inga-Karin did the drawings. It was the very first time she saw her own drawings printed!

We made this book out of our Venice experiences then and now. It might not have happened if we had not been lucky enough to have grownups who took us to that magical city when we were children.

We hope you will read about Vendela's journey even if you are not going to Venice just yet. Perhaps it will inspire you to go there someday, by yourself or with your children. And if you have no Uncle Ragnar with you, there is still a great deal in this book to tell you how wonderful Venice is.

Pages 88–93 contain lots of things that there was no room for in the story, with dates and reading suggestions and other nice bits. And on Inga-Karin's map at the beginning and end of the book are all the places visited by Vendela and her father.

Thank You

Uncle Ragnar and *Aunt Alice Lundberg*, who took Christina to Venice in 1953.

Inga-Märta Eriksson, Inga-Karin's mother, who took her to Venice in 1972.

Maria Brännström, who came along to Paris, to the Grand Palais, and to see the horses in 1981.

Andrea Johansson and *Kent Lundin*, who lent their faces to Vendela and her dad.

Marita Jonsson, a Venice specialist, who checked our book and told us about the dog that took the traghetto and other interesting things.

Marit Törnqvist, who got a salmon bone in her throat in Venice.

The nice doctor at Ospedale G. B. Giustinian who pulled out the bone.

Mika Romanus, who at the age of ten said she was going to take her children to St. Mark's blindfolded.

Daniele Rossi at Fornace Rosetto Estevan, Murano, who made us a glass unicorn.

Sivert Lindblom, the sculptor, who told us how the horses came to Blasieholms Square.

Professor Vittorio Galliazzo, who told us about his research into the horses.

Jean Minne, *Ingvar Gunnars*, and

Tomas Broman at Bergmans Konst-gjuteri, who let us watch while they cast a bronze horse.

Dottore Maria Da Villa Urbani, Procuratorio di San Marco, who told us about the horses and arranged for us to meet Professor Galliazzo.

John Millerchip, UNESCO-Private Committees, who talked about and showed us the capitals.

Architect Francesco Bandarin, Consorzio Venezia Nuova, who talked about the flooding and about Venice sinking.

Cesare Battisti, at the Venice tourist office.

Paolo Brandolisio, who showed us how he made *forcole*, the rowlocks for gondolas.

Publishers Luciano and *Franco Filippi*, who lent us old pictures of Venice from their archives.

Tord Andersson, at Restaurator, who showed us restored buildings in Venice.

Jan Sundfeldt, who let us into the secret of spaghetti.

Göran Österlund, who helped with photography, Bembo, and support.

Thanks also to *Contessa Lesa Marcello*, of the American group Save Venice Inc., and *Marina Montin, Satya Datta*, and *Giuseppe del Torre*.

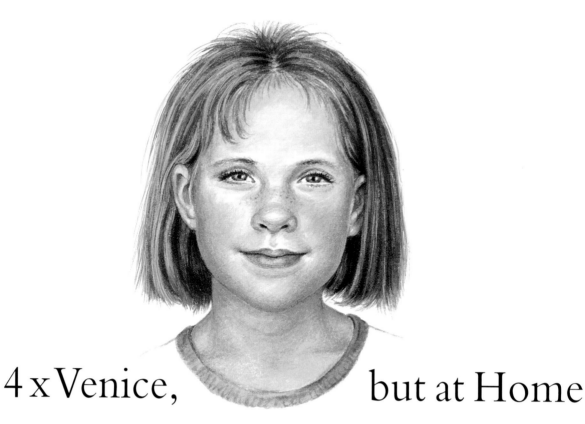

4 x Venice, but at Home

MY NAME IS VENDELA, WHICH I don't especially like. No one else is called that. If you rearrange the letters, it's almost like Lavender. I like that much better, though it's just as unusual a name. Lavender smells so good, and lavender blue is my favorite color. But I really want to tell you about something else:

I live in Stockholm, which is sometimes called the Venice of the North. That's because, like Italy's Venice, Stockholm is built on islands with water in between. The towns may not look alike in other ways, but there are things in Stockholm which are linked with Venice.

1. I'm thinking first of a square called Blasie-holms Square. It's large and long and almost always empty: no people, no cars, no shops. But there is something extraordinary there: two big horse statues, one at each end of the square.

I think ordinary horse statues, which often have a king sitting on the horse, look feeble and artificial compared with these. So I sometimes go out of my way just to say hello to "my" horses. My dad has told me that they are copies of horses in Venice. The real ones are gilded with real gold, and of course that's even grander.

I have discovered a lot of secrets about "my" horses, but not everything. That makes them even more mysterious. Many experts have done research on the horses for years. But as hard as they try, they haven't been able to work out how old the horses are. Nor where they come from, nor who made them. But they are very old. And before they came to Venice they were on a racecourse in Constantinople. That much is known. Terrible things have happened to them: they have been stolen again and again. Many great military leaders have wanted to show their power by becoming the owners of these particular four horses.

2. Another bit of Venice in Stockholm is the huge lion at the Historical Museum. It is a plaster copy of a stone lion in Venice. It is covered with graffiti, but the graffiti were made *nearly a thousand years ago.* Vikings from the Swedish county of Uppland had gone all the way to Piraeus in Greece, where the lion stood before it was taken to Venice as booty. And the Vikings scribbled, or rather cut runic letters, in the lion's body. Every time we go to the Historical Museum, we make a special trip to the lion.

3. From Granny I inherited a heavy paperweight in the shape of a stone slab with flower borders. The flowers and leaves are made of tiny bits of glass in different colors. It says VENICE on it, and one side is made of copper-colored glass which sort of shimmers. It was a present from Granny's grandmother, who had been to Venice. I often looked at it at Granny's house, and she sometimes let me hold it.

When she died, everyone was allowed to choose one of her knickknacks to keep in memory of her. I was last because I was the youngest, and I was worried that someone would choose the paperweight, but no one wanted it except me. What luck! I used to imagine that it was a replica of Granny's grave, with a border outlining the body in the middle, and one for each leg and one for each arm. The problem is that there is no border marking the head. Perhaps that doesn't matter. Granny is now in heaven, and her soul was probably in her head – but you can never be certain.

Great-great-grandmother's paperweight from Venice

A slice of Venice

4. One day Dad found some old issues of a magazine at an antique shop. They were from 1947. Every week, the magazine had a cutout page of slightly thicker paper. In three issues the sheets were called *A Slice of Venice*. You could stick on lots of cute little palaces with canals between them. There were gondolas, and tiny striped poles for mooring the gondolas. But it was all very small and delicate, so Dad copied the cutout sheets for me, in color, but a little bigger than in the magazine, so that it would be easier to cut out. I cut out every piece and stuck it on the map of Venice, so now I have *A Slice of Venice* in my room!

Driven Out to the Marsh Islands

DAD HAS TOLD ME ABOUT VENICE'S fantastic history. About the marshes and the small islands in the lagoon to which people are believed to have fled around A.D. 400. They had been driven out by other people who came to their country from the north: Attila with his Huns, Alaric with his Goths, and then probably Alboin with his Lombards as well.

Out here on the low-lying islands they built their houses on wooden piles, so they wouldn't get their feet wet. Gradually they strengthened the foundations of the houses with longer and thicker pilings. Hundreds of years passed and more and more people moved out there. They built better and better and more and more beautifully, and they traveled along the canals in long, narrow boats. The lagoon was full of fish and shellfish to live on.

The region was called the Veneto, and the people called themselves Venetians. They became expert shipbuilders and learned to build larger boats. Soon they could travel across the Mediterranean and even farther, and could trade with people in Africa and Asia. They brought back silks and spices and jewelery and sold them in Europe. One trader, called Marco Polo, made voyages of discovery as far away as China.

The Venetians established themselves as a separate state, with their own government, their own laws, and their own money. In time, they became a rich people. They built real palaces on the old pile foundations. Fortunately, the wooden pilings became as hard as stone deep in the mud in the water, where no air reached them. That was why they did not rot.

In addition to their wealth, the Venetians had a secret – a secret that many others wanted to learn, which I will tell you about.

I love going with Dad to the glassworks near where I live. You can watch the glass being blown. The glassblower picks up a lump of red-hot glass on one end of a thin metal tube. Then carefully he blows air in through the other end and he shapes the glass bubble with different tools. That's what the glassblowers in Venice did, but their glass became much more transparent than the glass blown in Stockholm. Besides, some Venetians had a special recipe for making mirror glass, and this was *secret*.

13

How About Going There …

 NE DAY WHEN DAD AND I WERE walking past "my" horses he said: "I think it's time for us to go to Venice, so that you can see the real horses, not just the copies. Anyway, every child should go to Venice," said Dad, "because Venice is a fairy-tale city."

"When can we go?" I asked.

"In the summer it's too hot and there are too many people. And in the winter it can be cold and wet. But during the Easter holidays I think it's at its best. We'll go then."

"Then I'll save up my allowance from now on."

Dad did some reading in advance, and so did I. We borrowed books on Venice from the library, and Dad bought a guidebook and a good map. We always think it's much more fun to go to a place if you know something about it. Otherwise, you risk missing the most extraordinary things. Especially in Venice.

The *Canal Grande* (which means "Big Canal") runs through Venice like a giant backwards S. And on our map we could see the *Piazza San Marco*, St. Mark's Square, where the horses are (but not on the map, of course). And a little farther on is the *Arsenale*, the military district where the scribbled lion guards the entrance.

We saw pictures of people traveling in gondolas – long, narrow black rowing-boats with the oarsman standing and sculling with a single oar. There are no cars in Venice, because there are no streets to drive on, only canals. Instead of buses, there are big motorboats, *vaporetti*, which run between designated stops. (It's one *vaporetto*, but several *vaporetti*.) And instead of taxicabs there are taxi boats – or gondolas. But there didn't seem to be any water bicycles.

The houses in Venice are very old and very beautiful. Along the Grand Canal, every house looks like a fairy-tale palace. (They never tear down old houses here!)

"A nice thing about Venice is that it's not very big," said Dad. "We can walk across it in three-quarters of an hour, or perhaps an hour."

"Where are their glassworks?" I asked.

"They are on an island outside the city," said Dad, pointing to the map. "It's called *Murano*."

"Do we go there by gondola?" I asked.

"No, gondolas are expensive. So we'll take a vaporetto."

One problem in Venice is that there are floods and the water rises unusually high. This is called *acqua alta* (high water). And Dad says Venice has been sinking a little every year. I don't dare to think how it might end …

We Come from the Sea

THE FIRST TIME YOU GO TO VENICE you should arrive by boat, Dad said, even if it's a little more expensive and takes a little longer. So, after landing at the airport, called Marco Polo after the explorer, we went down to the dock and took the boat instead of the airport bus.

When I stuck my head out of the boat window, a cold, damp wind blew my hair back. It smelled of the sea (and perhaps a little of the boat's exhaust). It got dark soon, because we had arrived very late in the afternoon, but it was a mysterious darkness – very exciting. We were on our way to Venice!

The boat ran along a route marked by piles, with occasional lamps reflected in the water. It was probably not very deep. Here and there outside the route hung fishing nets and other equipment you need for fishing. Smaller fishing boats were moving in different directions out there in the darkness. Here and there, muddy land stuck up out of the water. It looked really mucky.

"It's ebb tide now, low water," Dad explained. "In a few hours it'll be flood tide, when the water rises again and the lowest islands disappear. About six hours of high water and about six hours of low water, caused by the attraction of the moon on the water."

"What if we get *acqua alta*?" I said.

"I don't think that's going to happen this time of year. But you never know …"

Far out on the horizon, there was light. It was VENICE!

We stopped at various islands, but soon we were approaching the city itself. It was like sailing into the middle of a play. But everything was real, strangely enough. Some of the palaces were floodlit, but not for making a movie – it was a perfectly ordinary evening.

And there was the pink *Doge's Palace*, seeming to float on the water. This was where the doges lived in the past. The doge was the president (more

or less) of Venice. Beside the palace was St. Mark's Square, where the real horses would be …

When we landed, I thought: I'm taking my first step on Venetian soil.

"Can't we go and look at the horses right away?" I said.

"I think we'll go to the hotel first with our bags," said Dad. "We'll take the vaporetto."

That was very exciting, too. First we bought a vaporetto card which would last for several days, so we wouldn't have to keep buying tickets. We were going to take the Number 1 line from a floating boat stop. Ooh! It swayed under our feet with every wave. The boat came in and we climbed on board with our bags. We sat at the front, which has the best view, though it's also very windy. In front you have to sit, or the captain gets angry, because you block his view.

The boat turned in to the Grand Canal. It was even more extraordinary than I had imagined. Palace after palace along both sides, all "floating" on the water. That's how it looked, because the walls of the houses went straight down into the water. The front doors were well above water level. In front of the doors were striped poles for mooring your boat. In a few places there was a light in the window and I wondered who lived there. Princesses? Or countesses? Or ordinary people? And where were all the other people, the ones who lived in the houses with dark windows?

The first stop was on the left side of the canal by a big church with a round dome.

"It's called *Santa Maria della Salute*," said Dad. "We'll go there one day. I want to see some paintings there by an artist called Titian."

A Room with a View

THE NEXT STOP WAS ON THE right, but then the boat steered back to the left-hand side and there was our stop, called *Accademia*. We were going to stay at a little hotel quite close to the Accademia Bridge. That was good; it meant we didn't have to carry our bags more than a few meters from the vaporetto stop. Outside the hotel, steps went straight down into the canal. I saw that the water came up to the fourth step, counting from the top.

"Hurrah, our room has a view of the Grand Canal!" I said.

"Yes, that's what I asked for," said Dad.

The building itself was a little palace, although the hotel was quite shabby. We didn't have a TV or a telephone; the toilet seat fell off, and the faucet leaked. But our view was better than any TV, because it was real! Across the canal were other palaces. When I opened the window, I heard an opera singer singing "Santa Lucia" (in Italian, of course). And five gondolas came abreast, full of Japanese people. The opera singer was standing in the middle gondola, singing

The water came up to the fourth step

away, and an old man was playing the accordion for him.

"Shall we go and have something to eat?" said Dad.

"No," I said. "I have to sit here at the window and look out at the Grand Canal. Just imagine me sitting by the Grand Canal!"

"But you'll have lots of time for that later on," said Dad. "I'm hungry."

"I'm not," I said, lighting my travel candle. But the wind nearly blew it out.

Of course I went with Dad, hoping we could just go to the pizzeria on the ground floor of our palace, but that's not what Dad wanted to do.

Our part of the city is called *Dorsoduro*. We went to the edge of Dorsoduro, overlooking the island of *Giudecca*, and found several restaurants. We chose one where we could sit outside and we ate giant prawns on skewers with two different sauces (one was too strong). Good but messy, since you had to peel the fried prawns with your fingers. After dinner we walked a little way along the bank called the *Zattere ai Gesuati* and found a fantastic ice cream place. It had every flavor you could think of.

By then I was so tired we couldn't do anything more. I didn't even know how I would get back to the hotel. But in our room I couldn't help looking out at the gondolas and the palaces across the canal. It was really magical.

Fairy-tale city, yes. Dad says many writers have written books which take place in Venice. He thinks it is probably to give the authors an excuse to stay a little longer in such a fantastic place. But Shakespeare had apparently never been to Venice when he wrote his play called *The Merchant of Venice*. Though you never know.

And lots of artists have painted Venice and its canals. Dad said Claude Monet lived and painted in the palace directly across from us when he was in Venice. It's called the *Palazzo Barbaro*.

20

To the Horses!

WHEN I CAME OUT THE NEXT morning, I saw that the water in the canal had risen. It came up to the second step from the top.

"Shall we walk, or take the vaporetto?" asked Dad.

"We'll take the vaporetto," I said.

It was quite different seeing the palaces in the daylight. Some of them had cracks on the walls, and the paint was peeling here and there. But it didn't matter, they were still great. At the water's edge, the walls were often a murky green from seaweed. Our guidebook gave the names of all the palaces, on either side of the canal. Dad said it annoyed him, because he couldn't look at the book and at the palaces at the same time. So we decided to look only at the real thing.

And speaking of real things, there were masses of plastic bottles in the canal. Who would throw a bottle into such a beautiful canal?

Here and there, little birds swam about, but Dad didn't know what they were. As soon as I tried to photograph them, they dived and vanished under the not too clean water.

We got off the vaporetto near St. Mark's Square. But before we walked on to it, we were in the part of the square called the *Piazzetta*. This is a smaller square than a *piazza*. Dad showed me two huge stone columns which he said had been stolen from Constantinople. Between them there had been a place of execution, where they killed people who had been condemned to death for some crime. Even now, Venetians avoid walking between the columns. (We didn't, either, to be on the safe side.)

On top of the left-hand column is a statue of St. Theodore with a dragon (which looks like a crocodile). He was Venice's first patron saint. And on top of the right-hand column is St. Mark's winged lion, with its paw on an open Bible. The experts think the lion itself comes from China or Persia (stolen?), but the wings were added in Venice.

And now I must tell you who St. Mark was.

Mark's Mystical Miracles

MARK WAS SECRETARY TO PETER, one of Jesus' disciples. He listened to Peter while Peter was traveling around preaching Christianity. Then Mark wrote it all down and that became Mark's own chapter in the Bible, St. Mark's Gospel.

In pictures, Mark nearly always has a lion beside him. The lion has wings and rests its paw on an open book which is Mark's Gospel.

Peter sent Mark to Alexandria in Egypt and told him to build a Christian church there. When 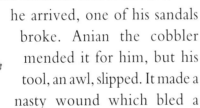 he arrived, one of his sandals broke. Anian the cobbler mended it for him, but his tool, an awl, slipped. It made a nasty wound which bled a great deal. Then Mark performed a miracle and Anian's wound healed instantly.

In time, Mark became bishop of the Christian community in Alexandria. But there were many  people who did not like Christianity at all. So they arrested Mark in the middle of the celebration of Mass in his church and killed him. His friends at least made sure that his body was embalmed. That means that it was treated with various chemicals so that it would not decay. Then his friends buried him in Alexandria.

Dad told me about the two Venetian merchants, Rustico and Buono, who sailed to Alexandria nearly eight hundred years later and stole St. Mark's body from his tomb. On the voyage home, they hid the body in a cargo of pork, knowing that the Egyptian police would never touch pork, because they thought pig meat was unclean.

When Rustico and Buono got back to Venice, the body was hidden in St. Mark's Church, inside a pillar near the altar. Only three people in the

whole world knew the hiding place; they were afraid someone from Alexandria would come and steal back the body.

Everyone in Venice was very proud to have such a famous saint as Mark for their church. So they decided that Mark would be Venice's patron saint. St. Theodore was almost forgotten, poor thing.

One legend says that while Mark was alive he was traveling one day between the islands which later became Venice and he met an angel who

said: *Pax tibi, Marce, evangelista meus.* That's Latin and it means "Peace be with you, Mark, my evangelist!" All the priests said the angel must have meant that it was ordained for Mark's body to stay in Venice. Did they make up the legend so that people wouldn't think it was shameful to steal Mark from Alexandria?

"Is Mark still inside the pillar?"

"No," said Dad. "The three people who knew the secret died without revealing it. Then no one knew where the body was. After many years, there was a fire in St. Mark's Church and people believed the body had been destroyed.

"But when the church was repaired, the doge and all the bishops and Venetian clergy gathered to pray to God that Mark's body would be found. And it worked. On the third day, June 25, 1094, they heard a terrific crash. A pillar had split and a human arm was sticking out. The doge and the priests decided that must be Mark, so he was laid to rest in the crypt, the area under the church. Later he was moved and placed under the high altar."

"Is he still there? Can we see him?" I asked.

"He can't be seen," said Dad. "And perhaps he's not even there, perhaps it's just a legend. But inside the church there is a picture showing the miracle of the pillar. And a plaque on the wall is supposed to show where it happened. When we go there, we can look for it."

Was it Mark's arm sticking out of the pillar?

25

Venice's Own Lion and a Toppling Tower

"THE LION OF ST. MARK BECAME the symbol of Venice," said Dad. "That's why you see winged lions everywhere. I don't think there are as many lions anywhere else in the world."

The square was full of pigeons, and people were selling small bags of grain. Masses of children and grownups were feeding the pigeons and photographing each other with pigeons on their heads.

"Do you want to buy some food for the pigeons?" asked Dad.

But I didn't. When the pigeons saw the grain, they flew up and ate from your hand. Whole flocks landed on people's shoulders and their heads. A pigeon in the hand may be all right, but ten in the hair is disgusting!

"That is the *campanile*," said Dad, pointing to an enormously high tower. "It used to be a watch tower, guarding Venice from its enemies – but do you know what happened at ten o'clock on July 14, 1902?"

"The enemy came?"

"No, the whole tower collapsed onto the square and the house next door. All that was left was a pile of bricks."

"Were there any people underneath?"

"No, oddly enough, not a single person was hurt," said Dad. "But the guard's cat died."

"What a shame," I said.

"Shall we go up the tower and look at the view?" asked Dad.

"Absolutely not," I said. "But where are the horses?"

The way it looked in 1902 when the campanile collapsed

The Wrong Horses

THERE THEY STOOD, FOUR NEARLY black horses up on the gallery over the front of St. Mark's Church!

"Dad! The *horses*!" I shouted, running. But it was impossible to run with all the pigeons around. So I held on to Dad's hand and pulled him forward to the church. We had to be careful not to step on any pigeons.

"Oh, aren't they great!" I said. (I meant the horses, of course.) "What a pity they're so high up. But they don't look as if they're gilded with real gold …"

"These are *not* the real horses," said Dad.

"They're not?" I said.

"No, these are just copies, too," said Dad. "The real horses can't stay out here, because the air is so polluted with exhaust gases that they would be destroyed."

"But there are no exhaust gases here! There are no cars."

"That's right," said Dad. "It should be very clean, but the wind blows exhaust fumes here from the mainland. And the boats don't always have emission controls. In the old days the horses stood out here, but when the air became too dirty the horses contracted 'bronze cancer,' a 'disease'

28

which eats holes in metal under the gilding."

"Won't we be able to see the real horses?" I said. "When we've come all this way!"

"They're in a museum now," said Dad.

"Oh, a museum!"

"No, not like an ordinary museum; they're in a room inside the church."

"Well, then, let's go," I said. "Now, right away."

We walked in through one of the church doors, but, oh dear, what a crowd lining up to see the inside. And a whole class seemed to be in front of us. We waited for a long time, but got no closer to the inside.

"We'll sit at *Florian's* for a bit," said Dad. It was sad to have to wait, but I knew that Florian's was the oldest and best café in Venice, perhaps in the whole world. But the sun had not yet reached Florian's side of the square, which is best in the afternoon. So we went and looked at the stands, which sold souvenirs as well as grain. Should I buy something? They were all selling more or less the same things. Cards to send home? A T-shirt with *Venezia* on it?

"Would you like a gondolier's hat?" asked Dad. They sold straw hats, too.

"Absolutely not," I said. "Not me. But the teddy bears probably would."

There were small gondolier's straw hats, teddy-bear size, and I chose two.

"Do you want two? One should be enough," said Dad.

"If I buy one for Gilbert, I have to buy one for Sullivan, too. Otherwise, it's not fair."

"What about Big Teddy? And Teddy Yellow?" said Dad.

"The hats don't come in their size," I said.

"But you don't want to use up all your money on the first day," said Dad.

So I bought only one hat.

Moors and Mosaics*

JUST THEN, A BELL BEGAN TO toll. A cloud of pigeons flew up in fright. We looked up. On top of a tower stood two black bronze men striking a big bell in turn with their hammers. On the wall below was a clock which showed not only hours and minutes but also the new moon and the full moon. On a "shelf" under the two Moors stood a gilded lion, as usual with its paw on St. Mark's Gospel.

And below, by the church, were two reddish marble lions which children kept climbing up and sitting on.

"Why don't you sit on the lion, too?" said Dad.

"Ugh, how touristy!" I said. "But I'd like a picture of the lion all by itself."

The lion was shiny and smooth from all the people sitting on it. It seemed to be really depressed, poor thing.

*Moors: Arabs from North Africa
Mosaic: Picture made of
small pieces of colored glass

30

"Look here," said Dad, pointing up to the church door farthest to the left. "You can see your horses represented in mosaic."

And there was a mosaic picture of the whole church, horses and all. I took a picture.

"What a funny idea," I said. "A church with a picture of itself on the outside. But they missed one thing."

"What?" said Dad.

"Well," I said, "to be correct, they should have a picture of the horses in their picture on the left door. And in that picture you should have the horses, too. And it should go on and on."

"I see what you mean," said Dad. "But perhaps it was too fussy to do that."

"Now at last we can go in to see the horses," I said. But, believe it or not, there were just as many people as before.

"We'll look at something else," said Dad.

"No," I said. "I can't wait another minute."

"But I want to show you something," said Dad, walking toward the Doge's Palace.

"I don't have the energy to go into the Doge's Palace," I said.

"I know, it's a little too big and not much fun for children," said Dad.

31

Cunning Capitals in the Doge's Palace

OW THAT I COULDN'T GET IN TO see the horses, I decided that I was going to photograph every lion I saw. You really had to keep your eyes open, because lions were hidden everywhere. The one on the tall column was too high up, it would be only a dot in the photograph.

But we found other, shorter columns. The Doge's Palace had lots, both along the Piazzetta and by the water. Farther up, on what is called the capital, there were carved figures – a lot of lions, in fact, if you looked carefully. The most fun was the third column from the corner on the Piazzetta. It had lions and other animals, too, all with food in their mouths: the dog had a bone, the cat a mouse, the bear a honeycomb, the fox a cock, and the wild boar a bunch of grapes! Dad lifted me up to take pictures of everything, but as he was putting me down he nearly dropped me – and I dropped my camera. But a man who was walking by managed to catch it just before it hit the ground.

"Thank you very much," said Dad in English. "My daughter was determined to photograph all the animals on this old column."

"Yes, they're really fine," said the man. "But in fact they're not that old. They were finished last year."

"Last year???" said Dad.

"Yes," said the man, who turned out to be an Englishman called Mr. Millerchip. "We had to make a copy of the old ones, which couldn't take the pollution. But you can see the original, I'm on my way there."

So we went to the Doge's Palace with Mr. Millerchip, but through a door that tourists are not allowed to go through at all (so perhaps we were not tourists anymore?). He was busy collecting money from different countries to repair damaged monuments and churches. We saw the dirty, partly eaten-away dog-cat-bear-fox-boar capital, and I photographed that, too.

"You can see which are the new ones outside," said Mr. Millerchip. "They are the whitest."

We thanked Mr. Millerchip and left.

The dog with a bone and the cat with a mouse on the new capital

Hunting Lions

"E'LL GO A LITTLE WAY AROUND, to the Arsenale," said Dad. "It's not too far. Then we'll go back and see if there are fewer people waiting to see the horses."

We crossed several canals on narrow bridges, but we stayed close to the water. We saw the *Ponte dei Sospiri*, the Bridge of Sighs, the bridge which all prisoners were forced to cross from the court in the Doge's Palace to the *Piombi*, the prison cells. We looked at the water and all the gondolas and all the vaporetti and taxi boats loading and unloading. And amid all the traffic swam the little birds, whatever they were. There were also the usual black-headed and common gulls.

Suddenly I realized that I was hungry, and so was Dad, so we stopped at a restaurant by the dock. Dad ordered sole, which is his favorite, and I had spaghetti, because that's my favorite. Dad thought the sole tasted like any old flounder, but the waiter said it really was *sogliola*, sole. Later we discovered that there are different kinds of sole and you have to find "Dover sole" on the

The Bridge of Sighs

menu in English to get Dad's kind. I had *tiramisù* (which means "pull me together") for desert. Then we went on to the Arsenale and looked for the lion. We almost didn't find it, because it seemed much smaller here than in the Historical Museum at home. And you could scarcely see the runic lettering at all.

"The museum at home says their copy is better," said Dad, "because the soldiers at the Arsenale have used the lion for target practice."

Dad asked a soldier standing on guard if there was a brochure or some other information about the lion. But all he said was: "Restricted area. Restricted area." So we gave up. The Arsenale has always been secret. It was where the Venetians built all their ships, and they didn't want to share that skill either. No ships are built there now, but it's secret all the same.

You can go absolutely lion-crazy in Venice. Over a door, on a door knocker, on a wall – I saw lions everywhere.

I finished a whole roll of film and we had to keep stopping for more pictures. It was worse when I spotted lions inside private courtyards. Then I had to sneak in and

The lion under me is the lion of
Piraeus. There is a copy in the
Historical Museum in Stockholm

ASSICVRAZIONI GENERALI

I managed to slip into a courtyard in St. Mark's Square to take a picture of the lion above me here

photograph them, too, although I was scared.

The lions made us take a long time to get back to St. Mark's, and when we got there at last, it turned out that we had been standing in the line to get into the church itself. The museum entrance was farther off, but – oh no! – the museum was closed. I was very, very upset.

Dad bought an extra teddy hat for Sullivan to comfort me. It didn't help much, I was too upset. We took the vaporetto home and I lay down on my bed.

"Here are your hats," said Dad. "Do you think they would fit Zephyr?"

"No," I said. But the hat did fit. Zephyr is my travel monkey, named after the monkey in *Babar*. I never travel anywhere without a travel monkey. I should have bought three hats …

Something **Awful** Happens

AFTER WE RESTED, DAD THOUGHT it was time to go out and eat. He had heard of a good restaurant not too far away in Dorsoduro, our part of town. On the way, we found a bar which looked cozy. You could stand at a counter and eat snacks on toothpicks. Dad had a glass of the bar's homemade wild-strawberry wine.

"Remarkable," said Dad. "It tastes *exactly* like wild strawberries."

He let me sniff it and taste a little on my finger. Yes, *exactly* like wild strawberries, especially if you closed your eyes. Sadly, there wasn't any wild-strawberry drink without alcohol, but I had *aranciata*, orange drink. I chose toothpicks with bits of sausage, and Dad had artichoke hearts and cheese. Everyone at the bar seemed to know each other; they didn't look like tourists. The little black dog sleeping beside a wine cask was definitely not a tourist.

When we came out, Dad found an old gondola work-shop on the other side of the canal (*Rio di San Trovaso*). We could see that they were building gondolas, and one was nearly finished. Making a gondola is very complicated, a real science, Dad explained. They have to use the best wood and they need precise measurements. The boat must be built slightly askew, larger on one side. That is to make it move straight ahead though the gondolier is standing on one side of the boat sculling with only one oar.

The gondola is painted painstakingly, with at least seven coats of black paint, to make it shiny and elegant. Dad told me that long, long ago gondolas were painted in all sorts of colors.

I got a postcard of the gondola yard at the bar that serves wild-strawberry wine. The bar is by the arrow

Then that was forbidden and they had to be black, because colors were much too showy. They also decided that women must not be showy either, and they were allowed only one necklace. After a new doge was installed, he removed the restrictions and Venetian ladies began to wear lots of necklaces again, but the gondolas stayed black.

We were looking for Dad's restaurant. We had to cross several canals and bridges and finally we walked down a little tunnel, a *sotoportego*, through a house, to get to it.

Dad ordered sole, of course, but the "right" kind. Then he managed to persuade me to have fish instead of spaghetti. But he shouldn't have done that …

I chose a salmon cutlet, because there are usually no bones in salmon. But there was in this piece. One bone. And it got stuck in my throat!

"Have a little drink," said Dad. "Perhaps you can wash it down."

But no, the bone stayed where it was. I went to the restroom and tried to cough and choke the bone out. That didn't work either. Now it really hurt. Dad looked down my throat.

"I can see it," said Dad, "but I can't reach it."

Dad called the waiter and showed him my salmon bone.

"Eat some bread, perhaps it will go down," said the waiter.

"No, I think it's really stuck," said Dad. "Do you know if there's a doctor near here?"

I started to cry, but crying hurt my throat, so I stopped.

"You're very lucky," said the waiter (unlucky, was what I thought). "If you cross the bridge outside the restaurant, there's a hospital on the other side of the canal. It's open around the clock."

Dad paid (the salmon was free), and we walked over to the hospital. A male nurse met us and took us straight to the doctor, who was a woman. She shone a light down my throat and took out some long forceps …

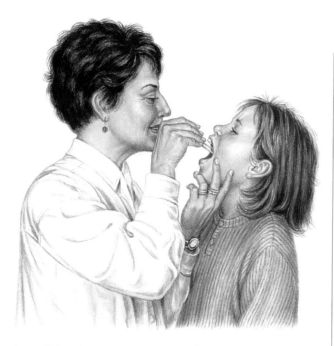

"Don't worry, open wide!" said the doctor, and coaxed out the bone. Ouch, it hurt. But it was quick, luckily.

"You were very brave, little *Occhi-Blu*," said the doctor. "It's a good thing you came in," she added. "You could never have swallowed that, and it would have been dangerous to try to do so."

Dad told me what the doctor had said, and that she had called me Occhi-Blu – Blue Eyes.

"How does it feel, Occhi-Blu?" asked Dad, and I nearly began to cry again. I felt very sorry for myself.

"Has she been vaccinated against tetanus?" asked the doctor.

"I don't know ... for sure," said Dad.

"It bled a little, so I must give her an injection. Is she allergic to anything?"

"No, not so far," said Dad.

"Now you must be brave again, Occhi-Blu," said the doctor, and gave me an injection in the arm.

It hurt much more than taking the bone out of my throat, but I didn't cry.

"I'd like you to come back in an hour, to be sure she has no reaction to the injection."

"Can she eat this evening?" asked Dad.

"Oh yes," said the doctor. "Something soft, like ice cream ..."

"And what do I owe you for your services?" asked Dad.

"Nothing," said the doctor. "It's a present from Venice."

We went back to the restaurant, and Dad ordered sole for himself and ice cream for me. Swallowing hurt a little, but the cold felt wonderful. So I had another one.

At last the hour passed and I did not have an allergic reaction.

"If only we had some flowers to take to the nice doctor," said Dad.

"Take this," said the waiter, and gave us a big bouquet from a vase by the restaurant entrance.

We crossed the bridge and went into the hospital. I carried the flowers. The doctor was there.

"Occhi-Blu is not allergic," said Dad. "And she has had two ice creams."

"*Mille grazie*," I said, giving her the flowers. (That means thank you very much.)

Diary and the Island of the Dead

THE NEXT DAY, MY THROAT STILL hurt. It felt just as if I had a cold, but it was only sore because of the fishbone. And my arm was tender where I had had the injection. We had meant to go see the horses, but I didn't want to go feeling like this, so we rested all morning.

I wrote postcards, which Dad had bought in the square outside. I wrote to Mom and told her about the horrid salmon bone. Dad thought she would be worried, so I added "But now I'm fine," though it wasn't completely true. For lunch we went down to the pizzeria in the hotel. I only had ice cream. Then I went back to our room and slept a little while Dad went for a walk.

When he came back, he said he had been to the Natural History Museum library and had asked about the little birds. (Typical of Dad; he always wants to know everything.) They looked it up in a book. It's called *svasso piccolo* in Italian and is a recent arrival in Venice. In Latin it's called *Podiceps nigricollis* and we can look it up in a zoological encyclopedia when we get home because the Latin names are the same all over the world.

And Dad bought me a very fancy notebook. *Travel Diary for Occhi-Blu in Venice from Dad*, he wrote in it. The book had a black-leather cover and a leather thong to close it. Best of all, the top of each page had a border showing the palaces along the Grand Canal – tiny pictures engraved in black and different on every page. The Venetians specialize in beautiful notebooks.

Travel Diary
for Occhi-Blu
in Venice
from Dad

My svasso piccolo

I began to write my travel diary at once. But in the afternoon my throat didn't hurt so much, so we made a *small* excursion: we took the vaporetto to an island called *San Michele*. I photographed a *svasso* on the way, but it must have been too far off.

That whole island is a graveyard. All you can see from the water is a pink wall around it. Dad wanted to look at some famous people's graves that were supposed to be there. We found lots of graves, but not the famous ones.

The graves in Italy are not at all like the graves at home. No grass, no flower beds, but often a photograph of the dead person and sometimes a little carving of something they were interested in. There is a special children's area in the cemetery. One boy had a soccer ball on his grave. And a girl who wanted to be a ballet dancer had a gilded ballet shoe on hers. There were lots of flowers on the graves, but not real ones – only china, plastic, or silk.

When we went back to the boat, I found a lovely silk ribbon in a wastebasket. Perhaps it had held some real live flowers, for a funeral. It was blue and absolutely clean and smooth, so I took it home.

I had mashed potatoes and ice cream for dinner. Back in the hotel room, I looked in the mirror to see if the sore spot in my throat showed. Then I saw that my hair was almost curly! I had always wanted curly hair.

"Dad, look, I have curly hair," I said. "Could it be the tetanus shot?"

"H'm," said Dad. "I think it's probably the air, it's so humid here. So your hair gets curly."

"In that case, I'm staying in Venice," I said.

At Last!

THE NEXT MORNING, MY THROAT didn't hurt but my hair was still a little curly.

We could go see the *real* horses! We wanted to be there when the museum opened at ten, when there would be fewer people.

The museum was on the first floor, but what steps, made for giants!

We bought tickets and went into a room which had postcards and books and souvenirs for sale. In the next room there was a gilded lion of St. Mark with its paw on an open book. *Pax tibi Marce evangelista meus*, it said. (It's fun to know Latin!)

And in the final room, the horses! Golden and magnificent against the white walls. And not *one* tourist had got there before us! We could admire the horses all by ourselves. Of course, there was a

45

glass barrier in front of the horses, but we were close enough. We saw the heads turned toward each other two by two, the raised hooves (they seemed to have no horseshoes), the short-clipped manes with the little knotted forelock tuft. The tails were also knotted at their ends. And what muscles; they must be so strong …

"But look, they're covered with scratches!" I said. "Does that look nice? Did someone try to scrape off the gold?"

"I don't know," said Dad. "Very curious. But in spite of the scratches they really look alive."

"Yes, they look as if they're moving," I said. "Or as if they had just moved and stopped. Or as if they're just about to move. But I'm sure they won't while we're here."

"No, probably not," said Dad. "And look, you can see the mark of a bit on their heads."

"Did you have a bit when you were in Constantinople?" I asked them, but the horses didn't answer.

"No, it would have been earlier," said Dad. "I read somewhere that they might have pulled the chariot of the Sun-God."

"And you're all patched up. That must be bronze cancer," I said. "Poor you, you needed a whole new back hoof."

"Take a picture of me in front of the horses," I asked Dad. "I wonder if they have names."

"Yes, there's a lot to wonder about," said Dad. "It's a pity there's no one here to ask. And there were no books about them in the museum shop. That was really odd. But they said we could ask at the bookstore behind St. Mark's Square."

I was quite sure I heard one of the horses snort!

Almond-Syrup Milk

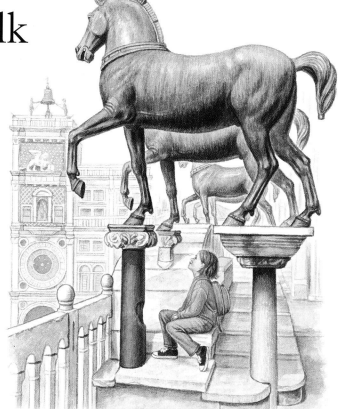

AFTER LOOKING AT THE HORSES from all directions, we went to the gallery where the copies are and looked out over St. Mark's Square. Seeing it from above was fantastic. You could tell who was feeding the pigeons because the area around them was black with birds.

We could also see the clock with the two Moors on the tower. It is said that when the clockmakers had finished the clock, their eyes were put out, so they could never make clocks as fine as this again. Yes, dreadful things happened in Venice …

After we bought some horse postcards and I made a quick last visit to the golden horses, we went down and got on line to get into the church. It is big. The ceiling and walls are covered with mosaics with gold all around. The pictures tell Bible stories, of course. Noah's Ark with all the animals was my favorite. My neck was aching; it was almost too much. But we never found the picture of St. Mark's arm sticking out of the pillar.

"Now we'll go to the bookstore and buy a horse book," I said.

And they actually had a horse book, but it was in Italian and huge and fat and too expensive, Dad thought. Though the pictures were great.

We found a restaurant where you could walk along a counter and point to the food you wanted. I liked that, because it meant no nasty surprises. Dad thought it was too busy. If you hesitated over your choice, a man said, "No stop, no stop!" to make you hurry. But I think children liked the restaurant; there were lots of them.

After the meal we searched for other bookstores, but they had no horse books at all. So Dad decided that we should buy the expensive book after all, for the sake of the pictures, even if he didn't understand much of the text. We bought some postcards of the inside of the church as well.

The sun had reached the Café Florian by now and we needed a rest. We sat down outside.

Curiously, Dad ordered tea, not his usual coffee.

"I think tea is more suitable here," said Dad. "They have their own blend."

Dad persuaded me to have *latte con sciroppo orzata*, because he wanted to know what it was. It was cold milk with almond syrup, which was wonderful if, like me, you like almonds (like liquid marzipan). Dad's tea arrived in two silver pots, one for the tea and one for the hot water (well, perhaps not real silver, but it looked very fancy). The almond milk came in a big glass with a "silver" holder. But it disappeared too fast.

It was fun to sit and watch people feeding the pigeons and taking photographs of each other.

Sometimes a whole group would cross the square with a guide well ahead, holding up an umbrella or a stick with a colored flag so the group would not lose her.

"Those are tourists," said Dad.

"Aren't we tourists?" I asked

"Yes, but not so many at once," said Dad.

"Let's pretend we're Venetians," I said.

The orchestra played and we sat at Florian's, watching the people and the pigeons and the arcades around the square. And the Moors struck their bell. And the campanile, the high tower, didn't fall. And the horses looked down on us from their gallery. And *I* was here!

Dad bought a postcard of the splendid floor of St. Mark's Church and I bought two postcards of Noah's Ark in mosaic

49

"If I ever have children," I said, "I'll bring them to Venice. And I will blindfold them and take them to St. Mark's Square and just before we get there I'll say: 'Now, children, you're standing in the world's most beautiful square!' Then I'll take off the blindfolds and they'll have almond-syrup milk …"

In the end, we had to go. But first we went to the restroom and we saw the inside of Florian's. It is very elegant, with red velvet sofas and little marble tables. Mirrors with gold frames and paintings of beautiful ladies, angels, and flowers completely covered the walls.

"We'll sit here and have hot chocolate if we come in the winter," said Dad.

If you wanted to, you could buy some of Florian's china. Dad bought the smallest cream jug (but it cost a lot). It had *Florian* written on it.

"This is for you, because of what you said about the blindfolds," he said.

I Am a Millionaire!

WE DECIDED TO WALK HOME IN-stead of taking the vaporetto. In spite of the crooked streets and the many bridges, it's not difficult to find your way, because there are small signs on the houses saying *Per San Marco* (to St. Mark's) or *All' Accademia* (to the Accademia).

We stopped often on the bridges and looked down at the water and along the canals. The houses were reflected in the water. Now and then gondolas glided by. Weird that they never collide! But gondoliers are very skilled.

Who lived here on the narrow canals? Often their cats sat in the windows looking out through the geraniums and the wash hanging on lines right across the canal.

"I think they do most of their laundry on Mondays," said Dad. "There was more washing yesterday." It was not very far to the hotel, but it took a long time, because you can never go straight, there's no straight way. And Dad wanted to go into all the stationery shops and look at notebooks and marbled paper. (They certainly are paper specialists in Venice!)

Dad also wanted to look in the windows of all the antique stores. Now I must tell you what we saw in one of them. In the very front of the window was a paperweight almost exactly like mine!

"We'll go in and ask what it costs," said Dad. "Just to find out what it's worth."

The man inside looked as if he was thinking, "You'll never be able to afford anything from this store!" when we asked the price.

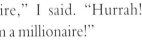

"One million six hundred thousand," said the man. "Very rare."

"*Grazie* (thanks)," said Dad. "We just wanted to know because my daughter has one at home."

"Did he really say 'one million'?" I asked when we left.

"Yes," said Dad. "He actually said 1,600,000! I must write that down so we can see that it's true."

"Imagine, I'm a millionaire," I said. "Hurrah! I'm a millionaire!"

"Yes, you're a millionaire. But in lire."

"How much is that in dollars?" I asked.

"Roughly nine hundred dollars," said Dad.

"Oh, well," I said. (Actually, nine hundred dollars wasn't too bad, either …) That evening I was so tired that we ate downstairs in the pizzeria. I had spaghetti Bolognese. As usual, we guessed where the spaghetti would begin to move when I stuck the fork in and began twisting it up. It looks spooky, because sometimes it begins to move right at the edge of the plate – try it! Yes, there are lots of good things about spaghetti.

Back in the hotel, Dad spent a long time paging through the heavy horse book, having dragged it home after all. He tried to read it, at least the picture captions. I sat by the window, looking out at the Grand Canal and all the gondolas gliding past. Suddenly I heard sirens, like a fire engine's. It was the fire-brigade boat setting out. I saw a police boat, too. Everything has to be done on the water in Venice.

"There's something about the horses' eyes," said Dad. "There's a lot about their pupils. And a lot about how they look inside. If only there was someone to ask …"

"Yes, and if only they had names," I said.

"In the book it just says Horse A, Horse B, Horse C, and Horse D," said Dad.

"Of course," I said, "those are short for …"

"… Alpha, Bravo, Charlie, Delta," said Dad.

"No horse can be called Delta," I said. "No, they'll be Adam, Bertie, Cesar, and David. From left to right. You know, I'm almost sure I heard a snort from Bertie when we were there. Well, not a snort – one of those horse sneezes. But maybe I imagined it …"

"Yes, you do wonder what happens in the museum when the clock strikes twelve," said Dad.

"Do they come to life then?"

"That's for you to decide, Occhi-Blu," said Dad. "Good night."

*This evening the water came
up to the last step from the top*

To Murano

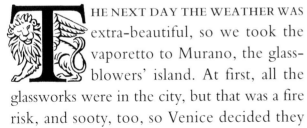THE NEXT DAY THE WEATHER WAS extra-beautiful, so we took the vaporetto to Murano, the glass-blowers' island. At first, all the glassworks were in the city, but that was a fire risk, and sooty, too, so Venice decided they should all move out to Murano.

Dad said glassblowing was regarded as a superior profession and glassworks were passed down from father to son. The training took ages: first you were an apprentice for years, then you could become a master. The masters knew how to heat up and melt a particular kind of sand in big ovens. And how you burned reeds and mixed the ashes plus something secret with the melted glass. At that time melted glass was often cloudy, but the Venetians succeeded in making their glass quite clear. It was called *cristallo*.

The glassblowers of Venice became famous, but so that the mirror-glass secret should not become known everywhere, they were forbidden to move from Venice. If they did, everything they owned was seized and their families were thrown into the *Piombi*, Venice's terrible prison. Murano itself consists of several islands with channels between. There were a lot of stops, but we got off at one called *Museo*, where there was a glass museum.

"Do we have to go to the museum?" I asked.

The museum was closed, because it was Wednesday, what luck! So we walked around looking at the glass shops instead.

I looked at paperweights, not like the one at home, but big glass marbles with flowers or patterns in various colors inside. I think they look so mysterious inside the glass. The most beautiful had only light blue – almost lavender-blue – flowers, but it was too expensive for me. When you turned it, it looked like a field of waving lavender inside. I would have liked that one, but I didn't have enough money.

I bought something else. The flowers inside the paperweights were made of glass rods in different colors, melted together. You could buy small slices or chips of the rods. I took a long time choosing and bought one glass chip (it was still too expensive).

The One-Minute Unicorn

SOME GLASSWORKS LET YOU come in and watch the workers blowing glass. It was very hot inside! The glassblowers went over to red-hot ovens and took up a blob of melted glass on their tubes. Then they would blow and turn and shape the melted glass with different tools, and suddenly there was a wine glass or the stem of a lamp or something else, which they put into another oven, not as hot. Glass has to cool slowly so that it doesn't crack. Each man made only one kind of glass object.

We stood and watched until a man in a suit came over to us. The boss, I think.

"Show the little girl how you make a horse," he told one of the glassblowers (in Italian).

"He's going to show you how to make a horse," said Dad.

"Oh, ask him to make a unicorn," I said, because I had seen one in a store.

Dad asked if that would be all right.

"I only do horses, not unicorns," said the glassblower.

The man in the suit pulled off his jacket. "I'll do it," he said.

And then, from that red-hot lump of glass, he blew and shaped a little unicorn. He drew out the legs and tail and horn with pincers, snip, snip, snip, and then clip, clip, clip, the mane was ribbed. I think it took about a minute .

"*Ecco* (here), it's ready," he said, standing the unicorn in front of us. "What is the little girl's name?"

"Here in Venice she's called Occhi-Blu," said Dad.

"Then you can have this, Occhi-Blu, but first it has to cool in the cooling oven. Otherwise, it might crack. It should be ready in three-quarters of an hour. Meanwhile, you can go and look at our glass exhibition in the shop upstairs."

"How kind they were to you," said Dad. "I feel as if we ought to buy something from them. And perhaps that was the idea. But oh, how expensive …"

"Where do you come from?" asked the man.

"*Sono svedese*," I said (meaning "I am Swedish").

"Then we will make you a special price because your queen has been here," said the man, showing us a photo of Queen Silvia visiting the glassworks. In the end, Dad found a pair of gold-rimmed champagne glasses which Mom was sure to like. And he paid the "special price," but it wasn't exactly cheap. Anyway, you had to remember the glasses were handmade in Venice.

"You can buy more next time," said the man.

And after three-quarters of an hour I got my unicorn. They packed it in a box with wood shavings so that it would not break.

Glass Chips

WE WALKED FOR A WHILE. THE church was closed as well (good!). Around a corner, it looked especially exciting, but it wasn't. The alley ended in a pile of garbage.

"Wouldn't it be wonderful if we found something ancient, like antique glass," I said, going closer. "Look, there's something sticking up out of the ground. A muddy little glass jar! Could I take it as a souvenir?"

Dad looked at it and saw *Pesto Genovese* written on it.

"No problem," he said.

We went into some more glass shops and in one of them I actually found a whole bag full of smaller glass chips in different patterns for the same price as my one chip had cost! That was very strange.

We ate lunch on the embankment and then the vaporetto came in. The stop was called *Navagero*.

We were just in time, and we got seats, too. More and more people got in,

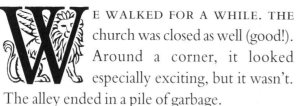

including a man with a big black puppy. It was very sweet and wanted to lick everyone's legs. Suddenly there was a great argument on the boat. The captain and the steward began to shout at the dog's owner, and lots of people joined in. Some of them were on the side of the captain, some the man with the dog. The poor dog looked unhappy.

Finally, we understood that the rules said the dog should be wearing a muzzle to get on the boat. The dog's owner refused to get off, but he wound the leash around the dog's nose. The dog looked even more unhappy.

That evening we ate at a nice place so small that it was not called a *taverna* but a *tavernetta*. We walked home across a big square called *Campo San Stefano*.

On the square there is a statue of a man whom the Venetians call *Caga libri* ("book-pooper"), because a pile of books has fallen down from under his coat, in the back.

On the way home, we looked for the

homeless cats in the little square by the Accademia Bridge. Yes, they were there tonight. Kind people had put out bowls of food for them.

Back in the hotel, I put one of the candles in the "antique" glass jar I had found on Murano. This time the flame was not blown out when I sat looking over the canal. I sorted my glass chips. There were 372 of them, 27 different kinds.

I found both dogs and cats at the bottom of Bernardo Strozzi's painting Feast at the House of Simon

The Dogs at the Bottom

THE NEXT DAY DAD SIMPLY HAD to go to the Accademia Museum and look at paintings.

"When you get tired, you can just cross the square to the hotel," said Dad.

There were too many rooms, I thought, and lots of paintings which were not too exciting. But sometimes a picture was of something I recognized. Like Tintoretto's *Theft of St. Mark's Body* or Bellini's *Procession in St. Mark's Square*, where

you could see the church and the horses. Here's a good tip: If you have to go to a big museum full of old paintings, you can just look at what is happening along the bottom of the pictures, about my eye level. There are often funny details, even on sad paintings. For instance, bright red little angels, food falling on the floor, rabbits scratching themselves, cats fighting, monkeys stealing fruit. The most usual seem to be little dogs. Yes, I always look for the dogs at the bottom.

They play for the dog in Pietro Longhi's The Concert

A little gondola dog in The Miracle of the Holy Cross at the Rialto Bridge *by Carpaccio*

A corner of The Rich Epicure *by Bonifacio Veronese*

Glorification of St. Ursula and Her Companions by Carpaccio. At the bottom the reddest angels I have ever seen. Carpaccio's signature is below them

"You must have a look at this," Dad would say. "This painting is *famous*." For instance, *The Tempest*, by Giorgione.

Dad talked about St. Ursula, who appeared in a series of paintings by Carpaccio. Poor Ursula, she went on a pilgrimage with eleven thousand maidens and the journey ended badly for everyone, but Ursula did become a saint.

Dad knows all about saints. He learned about them from his father when he was a child. In museums it can be very useful to know the saints. If the picture shows a man tied up, with a lot of arrows in him, you know it's St. Sebastian. He was shot full of arrows by two soldiers, but saved by a kind widow. Later, unfortunately, he was stoned to death anyway. (It's easier to become a saint if something awful happens in the end.)

And if there's a man with a sore on his thigh, it's St. Rocco. He caught the plague and the sore on his thigh is a plague boil. So as not to infect other people, he went off to the forest alone, and would have died if a kind dog hadn't brought him some bread every day.

But there were too many paintings of Madonnas and saints. I preferred Gabriel Bella's and Pietro Longhi's paintings, because they were of ordinary people at home, or at masked balls in Venice long ago. Masked balls are another Venetian speciality. Dad told me that each year during the Carnival in Venice lots of children and grownups wear masks in the streets. That's why you can buy masks in almost all the shops in town.

Dad wanted to visit some more rooms, so I went back to the hotel to write in my travel diary. I decided to try to write a horse diary.

FROM A
HORSE
DIARY

(Dad helped me a little with the diary, especially with dates and names.)

My name is Bertie and I am a very old bronze horse. I am almost entirely cast in copper, with only a little lead and tin, and gilded with real gold. I stand in St. Mark's Church in Venice with my three friends.

Adam is on my left. On my right are Cesar and David. They are as old as I am, and we four have always been together.

I can't begin my diary at the beginning, because we were born so long, long ago that we and everyone else have forgotten how that happened and when that was.

Some say we were made in Rome, perhaps two hundred or three hundred years after Christ. But we are almost sure that we are older, going back *before* Christ. We may have been cast in the studio of Lysippos in Greece. He was Alexander the Great's chief sculptor.

In any case, we were beautiful, everyone wanted us. Kings and emperors. But we ended up in Constantinople (now called Istanbul). It was the capital of the Eastern Roman Empire. I feel sure we were stolen; correct me if I'm wrong. In any case, it was Emperor Theodosius who decided that we should stand on his racetrack, the Hippodrome.

■VENICE

CONSTANTINOPLE■

Mediterranean

1203

Now I remember more: that year, 480 boats came all the way from Venice, with Venetian oarsmen and sailors, and French soldiers supposed to be joining the crusade in Jerusalem, to try to force people to become Christians. But they came here, instead. Weird, because here people were already Christian.

I can hear screams and the clash of weapons; in fact, I think a war has started. They say the foreigners are besieging the city.

The soldiers have taken over the whole city, though their commander is old, over ninety, and nearly blind. His name is Enrico Dandolo, and they say he has already sent two pigeons home to Venice with news of a great victory.

We hear we are to be loaded on board one of the Venetian vessels. It seems we are going to Venice.

"We must try to stick together," I tell my three friends.

We have succeeded so far. We are now on board Captain Domenico Morosini's ship. But they were so careless: Adam broke his leg; his left hind hoof almost came off.

1204

It was a long and dreadful voyage, with fierce storms in the Mediterranean. At last, we reached Venice.

Masses of people stood waiting at the dock. But when they unloaded us Adam's hoof came off alto-gether, and of all things, Captain Morosini stole the hoof (people are crazy).

Dandolo was extremely cocky about returning with so many riches. And he was proudest of all that he had us.

"I hereby present these horses, these masterpieces, to you Venetians!" he shouted.

And the people cheered and hung laurel wreaths around our necks.

No one considered that we were really stolen goods.

1254

They made a cast of my hind hoof, so now Adam has a new hoof instead of the old one. They did a good job. They say Morosini has placed Adam's old hoof over his door on Campo Sant'Agostin!

We know that we are to have a grand position here in Venice, on the gallery of St. Mark's Church. And we shall be allowed to stay together.

1792

We've been standing here more than five hundred years! We feel like real Venetians.

There is unrest in Europe. The ruler of France, Napoleon Bonaparte, wants to rule over

many countries. But Venice is trying to stay out of the war.

October 17, 1797

They did not manage to stay out of the war. French troops came to

Venice. Napoleon has defeated Austria, but in the peace talks he "gave" Venice to Austria. But first he made his soldiers take everything valuable home to Paris.

They decided to take Adam, Cesar, David, and me first of all.

December 13, 1797

We were hoisted down from our gallery. The people of Venice watched in silence. We were loaded on a boat, just as carelessly as before.

July 27, 1798

Napoleon organized a big parade through Paris with all his war booty. At its head, we four were towed along on an open cart by

two live horses (!). After us came some dromedaries (live), also stolen, poor things.

"I hereby present these horses, these masterpieces, to you Parisians!" shouted Napoleon.

1807

Napoleon had a huge triumphal arch built on the Place du Carrousel

to celebrate his victories. And we are to stand right at the top.

October 1, 1815
Napoleon has been defeated. The Austrian Emperor, Franz I, has decided that we must be given back to Venice. Hurrah!

December 13, 1815
The Austrian Emperor was there in person when we were handed over to the Mayor of Venice and the Venetians. At ten in the morning, we were towed on a barge from the Arsenale to St. Mark's and were welcomed by the people of the city. They fired a 21-gun salute. We were hoisted straight up to our gallery, and the people cheered. We were home again after exactly eighteen years!

August 29, 1902
It has been peaceful for nearly a hundred years, but I am beginning to feel poorly, especially the front leg I stand on. (Actually, it's quite hard to stand always on three legs.) Today my hoof broke off and I fell sideways. I'm going to master smith Munarotti to be mended.

April 24, 1903
Yesterday evening I was mended and hoisted up to my friends again. Just in time, because tomorrow is Mark's feast day, which we always celebrate in Venice.

May 26, 1915
World War I has broken out! This morning we were hastily taken down and moved inside the Doge's Palace (for safety).

December 1918
We traveled first by boat, then by train, to Rome (for safety). There we all stand, on the ground for the

first time, in the garden of a fine old palace.

November 11, 1919
The war is over. At 10:30 today we were back in St. Mark's Square, being hoisted up to our home.

December 1942
World War II is raging! We have to hide again so that no new ruler will steal us. But the cellar of the Doge's Palace seems to be good enough.

May 8, 1945

Peace!

World War II is over at last.

August 10, 1945

We are back on our gallery on St. Mark's Church! How lovely! We hope there will be peace and quiet now. No more wars, no more travels in the big world.

1965

We have been feeling ill for a long time, but it's only now that they have begun to examine us seriously. Specialists came from Rome and discovered that we had "bronze cancer." We had begun to rust and were being eaten away under the gilding. We had to go to the hospital. There we were X-rayed and microphotographed. We were washed inside and out with distilled water. When they knew all about our health, they started repairing us.

It seems we can't tolerate polluted air. Perhaps we shall not be allowed to go back to our gallery. Imagine not looking out over our beautiful square! But we'll just have to get used to it …

1977

They have arranged a fine room for us, with thermometers and hygrometers (to measure the moisture in the air), so that we shall always be comfortable and not get ill again.

They have put copies of us on the gallery of St. Mark's. From the square it's difficult to tell the difference, though the poor things are already dirty, and we are golden and gleaming.

The others were allowed to rest after their illness, but not me. I had to be shown at exhibitions all over the world. I went to Mexico City, New York, London, and Paris. Without Adam, Cesar, and David. It felt dreadful. We who had never been apart for two thousand years!

I thought the absolutely worst thing was going back to Paris – I have such bad memories of that city. This time I had to stand in a museum; there were now copies of us four on Napoleon's triumphal arch. And they're looking in the same direction, two by two, as if they were in some silly horse ballet.

1980

Home at last. Adam and Cesar and David were so worried about me!

Adam had said: "What if they keep him in Paris!"

But they didn't.

Tuesday, April 2, 1996

How time flies. Every day, masses of people come to admire us. Just today, a little girl was here. I thought there was something special about her – she was *really* interested. I mean, for a child. I think she believes we may be alive, though we were as still as we possibly could. Luckily, she doesn't know what we do after midnight …

Ugly Fish and Lots of Blood

HE NEXT MORNING WE GOT UP early, so early that we couldn't have breakfast in the hotel. It was cold and raw and rather misty. The garbagemen were rumbling up and down the bridges with their carts and emptying them into garbage barges.

We took the boat along the Grand Canal right to the Rialto stop. Just before it struck seven, we crossed the Rialto Bridge, which doesn't look like an ordinary bridge, because it has shops built along it.

On the far side of the bridge are the covered markets. The vegetable market was in full swing.

arranging all the fish on tables with chopped ice. There were lobsters and shrimps, and mussels, too. And strange sea creatures which we didn't recognize. Men came running along with wheelbarrows full of squid with the black ink running on the ground behind them. Then came wheelbarrows with huge tunas, several meters long, to be chopped in pieces. How the blood ran! Other peculiar, ugly fish also had to be cleaned.

Ugh, it was horrible, with all the blood and squid ink and all the entrails. And the smell! I decided never to eat fish again. Especially not squid.

Small boats pulled in at the canal moorings and loaded up with vegetables and fruit in great heaps. One heap got so high that I saw that … oh no … it was going to topple! But I didn't dare say anything. I was right, though: it toppled and the tomatoes tumbled out and turned into sauce.

We went on to the fish stalls, where they were

"Now we'll go down the canal again, and then we can have breakfast," said Dad. Breakfast – no, I didn't want to think about it.

"And then we can visit a tiny museum," Dad went on.

"Museums today, too? In that case, the horse museum again."

"We might be able to do both," said Dad.

"Oh, it's Good Friday today," I said. "All the museums will be closed."

We took the boat back along the Grand Canal, past St. Mark's and the Doge's Palace, and got off at the stop called *San Zaccaria*. There we ate breakfast at a big hotel. At first I didn't want any, but when Dad's breakfast came, I changed my mind.

Then we took twists and turns, looking for the *Scuola di San Giorgio degli Schiavoni*. A complicated name. Up and down bridges reflected in little canals. Into alleys which ran straight into the water. Lucky that we had a map!

Walking down one wrong alley that led nowhere, we discovered a workshop where a man was making a *forcola*, a gondola rowlock.

The workshop was full of half-finished rowlocks,

beautifully sculpted and polished. They looked like modern sculptures.

We were told that every gondolier had to have a rowlock that was to his liking. It was as important as having shoes the right size, said the carpenter (perhaps I should call him the sculptor).

A Dragon and a Very Small Dog

In Carpaccio's painting, St. George is sticking his lance right through the dragon's head. The princess is standing at the far right, praying to be saved. Even if it doesn't show, her heart must be thumping

AT LAST WE FOUND THE MUSEUM. It was open, and it really was tiny. Just inside the door hung a black cloth and we had to pay a man standing in the dark. We were given an unusually fancy ticket. At first we could barely see, but then our eyes got used to the half darkness. All the paintings in the room were by Carpaccio. And with his paintings, the longer you look, the more exciting details you find.

Some paintings were of St. George and the Dragon. Dad says St. George is invented, but in the legend he came to a city ruled by a dreadful dragon. It had eaten up all the cattle and it demanded two young people for lunch every day. The dragon's disgusting leftovers were every-where.

But just as it was about to eat the king's daughter, St. George came and pierced it with his lance. The blood spurted out, and though the dragon did not die, it lost its power.

In the next picture St. George has it on a leash and the dragon is being humiliated in the market square with the lance through his head.

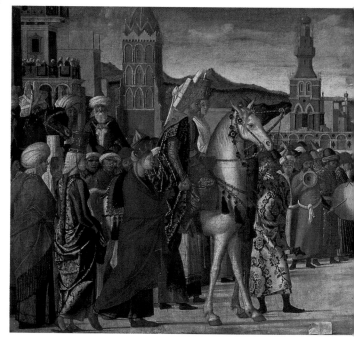

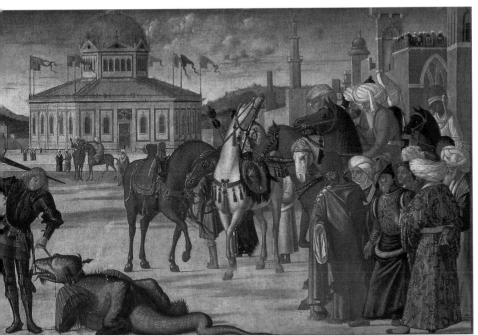

Is St. George going to cut off the dragon's head?

No, the legend says that from that day on the badly wounded dragon followed the princess as faithfully as a dog on a leash

73

"Look, a lion," I said, pointing at another painting. "Is that St. Mark and his lion?"

"No," said Dad. "That's not Mark's lion, it has no wings. That is Jerome's lion. St. Jerome (*Gerolamo*, in Italian) lived alone in the desert for three years so as to be able to think and read and become a better person. There he met a lion which had a thorn in its paw. Jerome pulled it out and they became friends for life.

In the next picture he arrives at a monastery with the lion, and all the monks are terrified. And the next shows Jerome's funeral, with the lion grieving in the background.

One painting showed another saint, Augustine, in his study. He is actually writing a letter to Jerome. And at that moment he thinks he hears Jerome's voice. But the main subject is definitely the little dog sitting in the middle of the floor. He must have heard the voice, too. (If you look closely at the shelf along the wall, you can see a

Here comes Jerome with his friendly lion, but the monks are running away

Carpaccio signed his name on the piece of paper in front of the dog

horse there, almost like one of the horses at St. Mark's.)

"Carpaccio never just wrote his name in the corner of a painting when it was finished," said Dad. "He painted a book or a piece of paper somewhere in the picture, with his name on it. The paper is often so skillfully painted that it looks real. That's called *trompe l'oeil*, which means 'deceive the eye' in French."

We went out into the sun again. Then we heard a sound: "Wuff! Wuff!" it went. Or rather, "Wiff! Wiff!"

There was Carpaccio's little dog, running along, attached to a big fat man. Wasn't that weird?!

The Secret of the Horses' Eyes

ROM THE CARPACCIO MUSEUM IT was not a long walk back to St. Mark's Square. We climbed the massive steps to the horses again and bought new entrance tickets. This time we were not alone. There were lots of tourists and there was a man inside the barrier near the horses' tails.

"I wonder what he meant," said Dad. "That Galliazzo who wrote our big book. About the eyes and the pupils and the sun … and the scratches …"

"Yes," I said, "and I'm still wondering about the horses' names …"

"Let's go and ask," said Dad. My dad always wants to know everything.

At the ticket counter they did not know.

"No, we know nothing about scratches or names," said the ticket seller.

"But is there really no one we could ask?" said Dad.

"No," said the man. "Well, perhaps. You could try Professor Galliazzo from the university. He's here today taking measurements."

We went straight in again.

"*Buon giorno*," said Dad. "Do you speak English?"

"No, no, but French or Italian are all right," said the professor. "*Mi dispiace.*"

"Excuse us for bothering you," said Dad in French, "but we understand that you are the Professor Galliazzo who wrote that fantastic book about the horses. We've just bought it."

"That's wonderful," said the professor.

"We were wondering about all the scratches," said Dad. (How did he know what "scratches" is in French?)

"Yes, I wonder, too," said Galliazzo. "Perhaps they thought the gilding made them too shiny."

"Do the horses have names?" I asked.

"Well," said Galliazzo. "I usually call them A, B, C, and D, from left to right."

What sad names! Who wants to be called D? Adam, Bertie, Cesar, and David are much better.

"Have there been any new discoveries about the horses' age and origins?" Dad asked.

"No, nothing definite," said Galliazzo. "But I have my theories. Others have theirs."

"So what do you think?" asked Dad.

"I favor a Greek origin," said Galliazzo. "Perhaps between the early 300s and the mid-200s. Before Christ, that is. And I believe they pulled a sun chariot with a sun god in it. We know Lysippos used the same casting technique for horse groups."

"How can you know that?" asked Dad.

"I have spent five whole days inside the horses," said Galliazzo.

"Inside?" said Dad.

"Yes, I've photographed every centimeter inside to study the casting."

"Ask him how he got in," I said.

"The heads come off," said Galliazzo, pointing to the "collar," "and I had a little stepladder to climb up. It was uncomfortable sitting there, *molto brutto …*"

Now and then the professor got so excited that he began to speak Italian.

"But what did you mean about the sun and the reflections in the pupils?" asked Dad.

"Well, I found that the pupils' reflections are different in the different horses," said Galliazzo. "The sculptor assumes that the sun shines on the horses directly from behind. So the reflections in the two left-hand horses' eyes are a little different from those in the two right-hand ones. And that makes me think that two of the horses' heads changed places. A and D quite simply changed heads."

Dad translated for me.

"No, no!" I said. "I don't like that! The great thing is that they don't look in the same direction like trained circus horses."

"I agree with you," said Galliazzo. "*Come si chiama?* What's your name?"

"Occhi-Blu," I said. "Promise not to change their heads back again!" (Dad translated.)

"Yes, I can promise that, Occhi-Blu," said the professor. "The horses have gotten used to looking like this."

"Thank you so much for taking the time to answer all our questions," said Dad. "*Di niente,*" said Galliazzo. "It's especially nice when children are interested."

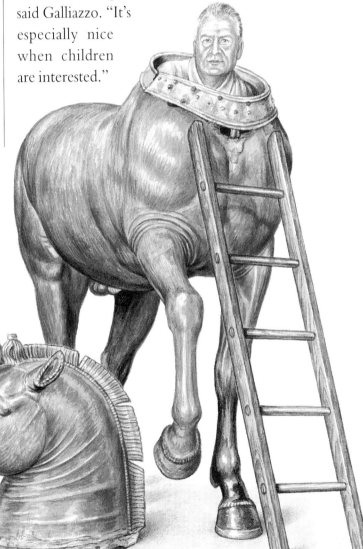

Do You Have a Bellini Junior?

DAD THOUGHT WE SHOULD TAKE A break at *Harry's Bar* after everything we had done today. It was right next to the *San Marco* vaporetto stop.

"Is there something special about the bar?"

"Hemingway, the author, used to go there," said Dad. "And it started in a funny way. A bartender at a big hotel in Venice was called Giuseppe Cipriani. Harry Pickering was one of the regular customers and he was American. One day he was broke. He had no money to pay for his hotel room or the tickets home for him and his black dog, a Pekinese.

So kind Cipriani lent him money, $5,000, a lot of money to lend to a customer. Pickering went home to the United States, but no money came. Finally Cipriani lost hope.

78

"Two years later, who should be standing in the door but Harry Pickering!

"Here are $5,000," he said. "Thanks for the loan. And for being so enormously kind, lending me money when I needed it so badly, here's another $20,000. But on one condition: you buy yourself a bar, and we call it Harry's Bar."

"And that's what Cipriani did," said Dad. "He even called his first son Harry, *Arrigo* in Italian, after Pickering. And now it's Arrigo who owns the bar."

We ordered a *Bellini* for Dad and a child's Bellini for me. A Bellini is a mixture of the best peach purée and white sparkling wine. A Bellini Junior has a soft drink instead of wine.

On the wall, low down near the floor, I found a small winged brass lion which I photographed. The waiter who served us asked if I knew what sort of lion it was.

"It's St. Mark's lion," I said.

"That's right," said the waiter. "But do you know why it's in that spot? It's because when there was an *acqua alta*, a flood, in November 1966, the water came right up to that point."

"But if the water came up to here," I said, "what about the bar? Tables and chairs must have been floating around and …"

"Yes, the bar was ruined and had to be

St. Mark's lion on the wall

repaired," said the nice waiter.

Dad told me that the 1966 flood was the greatest ever, but that there can be floods in Venice between October and April with such force that the ground floors of the houses are flooded and people have to hoist their furniture up to the roof. And sometimes you can row gondolas on St. Mark's Square. That's why there are always stacks of boards there, to be put down for people to walk on when there's a flood.

The bad thing is that there are more and bigger floods in Venice every year. There used to be perhaps *one* bad flood a year, then there were ten, and, in 1997, there were ninety-nine. But the water has never been as high again as in 1966. Not yet …

An old photo of acqua alta *in St. Mark's Square*

Help, Venice Is Sinking!?

FLOODS DEPEND ON SEVERAL things," Dad explained.

"First, there's a wind called *sirocco*. It blows water in from the sea to the shallow Venetian lagoons. Another wind, called *bora*, stops the seawater from flowing back out to the sea. If the two winds coincide just as normal high tide arrives (the one that depends on the moon), there is flooding in Venice.

"The usual moon high-water is not dangerous. It's quite useful to Venice. It means that fresh seawater gets into all the narrow canals; otherwise, they would get stale and stagnant."

"But why are there more floods now than before?" I asked. "The moon and the winds have always been there, haven't they?"

"Well, it's because of several things," said Dad. "They have dug the canals deeper for bigger boats. Then more water can rush in. They have also made barrages and drained off the land, so the water has much less space to spread into when it's flooding in. But the most serious is that all of Venice has been sinking."

"How awful!" I said. "Why is that?"

"It's because of all the heavy industry on the mainland," said Dad. "Industry needs lots of freshwater, so they have been pumping up groundwater from deep down in the earth, below the seabed. And as that has emptied away, the seabed has collapsed and sunk lower. And Venice has done, too, of course."

"But it can't go on like that," I said. "I want to bring my children to St. Mark's Square! What if it's under water by then! Can anything be done?"

"Yes, it can," said Dad. "Industry has already

been forbidden to take any more groundwater. All freshwater is now coming in pipelines from the Alps. But land is still sinking several centimeters each century in this part of the world. And the Mediterranean is rising a little."

"No, stop, don't say that!"

"Some people put their trust in groundwater flowing back into its original sources below the seabed. Perhaps this could raise Venice a little," said Dad. "It may also be possible to build three huge water gates."

We saw from the map of the whole lagoon how it could be done. Outside the city there are two long, narrow islands in a line, *Pellestrina* and *Lido*. At each end, the islands almost reach the mainland, where it sticks out toward the islands like two narrow tongues.

"They have already built a high marble wall right along Pellestrina to protect the island from the sea," said Dad. "So Venice can be flooded only through the two openings between the islands and the mainland and the third opening between Pellestrina and the Lido. As soon as the water looks too high, they would only need to close the gates, and then open them again on the all-clear."

"Why don't they build those gates right away?" I asked, of course.

"The politicians never agree," said Dad. "Some think it would damage the seabed and stop the clean seawater from flushing the channels. Others believe that you can save Venice only by refilling the canals that have been dug for big ships and allowing the lagoon to recover its original rhythm. But then it would be more difficult for the big supertankers to come through and unload their oil in the mainland harbors."

"But are supertankers really allowed here?" I asked.

"Yes, strangely enough," said Dad. "Just think if two of them collided and the oil ran out … all of Venice would be destroyed."

"The oil ships must go a different way, or better still go to another place," I said, "and industry must move there."

"But that may not be what the people who work there want," said Dad.

"That's what should happen anyway," I said. "They can't want to live among oil spills. Just think of *svasso piccolo*! I'm sure all the birds are against supertankers."

The Dog 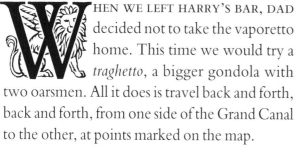 and the Traghetto

WHEN WE LEFT HARRY'S BAR, DAD decided not to take the vaporetto home. This time we would try a *traghetto*, a bigger gondola with two oarsmen. All it does is travel back and forth, back and forth, from one side of the Grand Canal to the other, at points marked on the map.

So we walked toward home, the same way as on Tuesday. (The million-lire paperweight was still in the window.) But at *Campo del Traghetto* we went down to the canal and climbed into the long gondola. You stand all the way. It was wobbly, with lots of backwash, but all the passengers stood anyway. And I held on to Dad. It only cost about thirty-five cents.

Dad had read in a book that a dog who lived at this exact spot took the traghetto across the canal alone every day to visit the dogs along the Zattere docks. Then he took the traghetto back again. He thought it was too tiring to walk up and down the high Accademia Bridge. Once a week, the dog's master paid his fares for the whole week. We looked for the dog, and we did see two dogs playing with a ball at the traghetto stop, but he probably wasn't either of them.

When we landed at Dorsoduro (our part of town) Dad, who never gives up when he's traveling, said, "Now we can go see Titian's paintings in Santa Maria della Salute."

Oh no, I can't, I thought. But luckily they had already closed the church, as it was late, so Dad missed Titian.

I dragged myself home. It wasn't far, but walking up and down four bridges felt like ten kilometers. Back at the hotel, I lay down on the bed and instantly fell asleep.

The Last Evening

WHEN DAD WOKE ME LATER THAT evening, I didn't think I could move, much less get up and go out. But it was our last evening, so I did. I even put on my dress, the lavender-blue one. And that silk ribbon I found on the cemetery island … should I wear it as a hair ribbon in my curly hair? No, it looked stupid. It was too short for a belt … but would it go around my neck?

Finally, I knotted it around my leg. It looked quite nice, though a little unusual.

First, we went to the nice bar and Dad bought a bottle of the wild-strawberry wine for Mom, to inaugurate the Murano glasses with. Then we went back and crossed the Accademia Bridge. We stopped at the top of the bridge and looked down the Grand Canal at the vaporetti landing below and at the sour-looking lions on the railing of the garden on the other side of the canal. (I had already photographed them.)

"That's where we live," said Dad, pointing to our window.

"But not for long," I said, sighing.

"And we haven't seen any cars or TV for a whole week!" said Dad.

Below the bridge, on the other side, by the little garden, we looked for the usual cat gang, but we didn't see a single cat.

We walked to our tavernetta, called *San Maurizio* after a saint whom Dad has never heard of. To get there, you pass the most fantastic candy store I've ever seen. As it was our last evening, I was going to buy some chocolates to take home. The problem was choosing. There was toffee and nut chocolate and flaked almonds and truffles. There was pink and blue and green and white chocolate shaped like masks. And caramels and *wonderful* pillboxes. And of course, Easter eggs and chicks and lambs and rabbits in marzipan. And a whole section of pastries as well.

"I can't decide," I said.

But in the end I chose masks in different colors and four pillboxes (one for my best friend, Annika, one for Mom, one for me, and an extra one). Then we went to the tavernetta and found an empty table by the counter. I ate only good things that I could point to at the counter, four different first courses – and of course Dad ordered Dover sole.

I didn't want to talk about going home tomorrow. So we talked about my curly hair, and how the horses were right now, and what we would do next time we came.

"What if Venice is all flooded next time we come?" I said. "What if everything has sunk into the sea."

"No," said Dad, "it won't go that quickly. Everything will be here next time, I promise."

We walked slowly home. It was dark and the streetlamps were lit. The evening light in Venice is especially beautiful, because there is pink glass in all the lamps.

At Campo San Stefano there were still lots of children playing around the book-pooper's statue. And at the Accademia Bridge we saw that our cats were back. Someone had put out bowls of food for them again.

We stood on the center of the bridge for a long time, looking up and down the Grand Canal. One or two gondolas glided by.

"Oh no," said Dad. "We've forgotten …"

"Not the candy bag, not the bag with the wild-strawberry wine," I said.

"No, but we've forgotten to ride in a gondola," said Dad. "Can you forgive me?"

"Oh well," I said. "We'll do it next time."

"We'll have a farewell ice cream instead," said Dad. So we walked across our island, and along the waterside. The pink streetlamps were very comforting, and the ice cream was delicious. I had pistachio. As we walked home, a wind rose and the water splashed over the side, because it was high tide. At the hotel it almost reached the *top* step … What if it rises even higher?

How Can a Week Pass So Quickly?

THE NEXT MORNING IT WAS TIME to go home. The only good thing was that the water had sunk down to the lowest step.

We took the vaporetto on a farewell trip along the Grand Canal, said goodbye to all the palaces and one or two little *svassi*. Just before the Rialto Bridge, I saw a big rat running up a molding outside a house right above the surface of the water. We went under the bridge, past the market stalls, past the church where St. Lucia is buried, and past the dreary railway station to the terminus at *Piazzale Roma*, where we got off.

I had a real shock. Help, there were cars and buses rushing to and fro, it was dangerous! And what a noise and smell! We had become completely unused to traffic this week.

We took the bus to Marco Polo, the airport. It cost less than a tenth of what our airport boat had cost, but we had to stand quite a bit and it stopped at lots of stops to let people off. At least we sat for the last part.

We had a little Italian money left, so Dad bought *Parmesan cheese*. But he should have done it in the city instead, because it was much more expensive here. And he bought *Bacci*. That means kisses; they are nut-chocolate balls with a proverb in each.

I bought a wife for Zephyr with the last of my money. She has black fur and a pale face with fur edging. She is very pretty, though she has two right arms instead of one of each. But that might be quite practical … In any case, it made her a little less expensive. I named her *Serenissima* (Serene Highness) after the Republic of Venice, which is sometimes called that.

My hair was so nice and curly when we got on the plane! But by the time we landed, it had straightened out in the extra-dry air on the plane.

Zephyr and his Serenissima

My Journey to Venice is over

P.S. 1

Guess what I got for my birthday? Yes, the paperweight with the lavender field inside. Dad had bought it without my seeing.

P.S. 2

The name of the *svasso piccolo*, the little bird we saw in the canals, is "black-necked grebe." On migration or in hard winters they turn up in estuaries and coastal waters in Britain, but breeding pairs are quite rare. They fly south in the winter and now some have arrived in Venice. This is how it looks in the winter. (You can see the summer plumage on page 81.)

Things You Might Like to Know

Here are some things it may be fun to know if you're going to Venice.

Or Stockholm. Or nowhere at all. At the end is a book list and lots of dates.

Italian language hints

Read the pronunciation rules in the front of an Italian-English dictionary. *C* is pronounced *k* except before *e* and *i*, when it is pronounced *ch*. *Casa* (house) is pronounced *kasa* and *cento* (one hundred) is *chento*. Useful when you order food or ask directions. *Doge* is pronounced like *dough*, ending in a soft *g* like garage. Most dictionaries have a section of common phrases. *Thank you* is *grazie*. *Sorry* is *scusi*. *How much* is *quanto costa*.

Easy, and difficult, to find the way

The inner city has six sections: *San Marco, Castello, Cannaregio, Santa Croce, San Polo*, and *Dorsoduro*. And the island of *Giudecca*. The doors are not numbered by streets. Each city section is numbered from one to several thousand, so it's sometimes tricky to find the right door number.

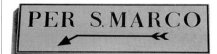

Luckily, there are little signs here and there showing the best way to all the important places in Venice. But you must have a good map. You can buy one at any bookshop or get it free at the new tourist office, situated in the arcade of the south-west corner of St. Mark's Square close to Calle dell' Ascensione. Make sure to ask for a colored vaporetto map or you'll get a little black–and–white one. The city may be small, but the alleys twist and turn and it can feel like walking through a maze. A compass can be helpful.

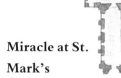

What's happening in Venice?

At most hotels (sometimes at the tourist office) you get a free booklet called *Un ospite di Venezia* (A Guest in Venice). It lists opening times for museums, banks, and shops, and all the events for that month.

Fewer and fewer Venetians

In 1966, 123,000 people lived in Venice. By 1995, there were only 72,000. Young people move: problems with work and high rents. Schools close because there are so few children. People live at *Mestre* on the mainland now and come to Venice by day to work. But ten million tourists came in 1994. The figure rises every year. Most come in June, July, and August, when there is one-way traffic for pedestrians on roads and bridges.

So don't go then!!!

Miracle at St. Mark's

(Pages 25, 48) The position of the mosaic showing Mark's arm in the cracked pillar. It looks more like a cupboard door opening.

The collapsing campanile

(Page 26) Many books have photographs seemingly taken just as the tower fell at 10 a.m. on July 14, 1902. Of course, we wanted one for our book. But all the photos we saw looked touched up. We did try to buy a wonderful picture from the shop of Zago, the photographers, who had the copyright, but they thought we were being a nuisance. We could not find out if the picture was genuine or a fake.

Anyone passing Zago's showcase can take a look. It's on the wall in Calle dell'Olio near Campo San Aponal, San Polo district. They were more friendly at Filippi publishers; they own vast numbers of old black-and-white photos from the 1800s and early 1900s and gladly let us show their falling tower.

Filippi's toppling tower

Santa Lucia is buried in Venice

(Page 19) Lucia, a rich lady from Syracuse in Sicily, gave all her wealth to the poor. She refused to marry, but gouged out her own eyes and sent them to one of her suitors. They tried to burn her at the stake, but the flames fell back. They finally killed her with a sword.

She was buried in a church in Venice named Santa Lucia, but that was torn down to make way for the railway station. She was moved to another church, San Geremia. The station is still called Santa Lucia after her.

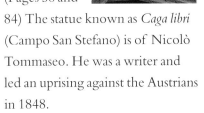

The book-pooper

(Pages 58 and 84) The statue known as *Caga libri* (Campo San Stefano) is of Nicolò Tommaseo. He was a writer and led an uprising against the Austrians in 1848.

Venice, city of masks

Forty days before Easter, many people wear masks in Venice. One mask is called the *plague doctor*, a white face with a long beak. When plague raged in Venice, a doctor invented the mask. He wore a gown which had been waxed and had a hood and a black hat. Inside the beak he had garlic, to avoid the smell of the sick. He lifted their sheets with a stick, to escape infection. *Mondo Nuovo*, Rio Terrà Canal near Campo Santa Marguerita, Dorsoduro, is a good mask shop.

About gondolas

In the 1500s there were some ten thousand gondoliers in Venice. Now there are only four hundred. The profession passes from father to son (no women gondoliers yet) and is well paid after ten years' apprenticeship. The gondolier stands on the poop and rows or, rather, sculls on the right, with one oar.

That's why gondolas are lopsided, twisted slightly to the right, so as not to go around in circles. They are 11 meters long, 1.4 meters wide, and weigh about 500 kilos. Gondolas are

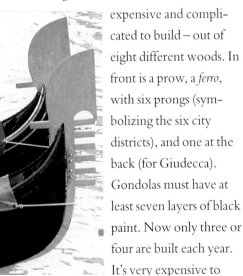

expensive and complicated to build – out of eight different woods. In front is a prow, a *ferro*, with six prongs (symbolizing the six city districts), and one at the back (for Giudecca). Gondolas must have at least seven layers of black paint. Now only three or four are built each year. It's very expensive to take a gondola. The fixed price is in *Un Ospite di Venezia*.

About vaporetti

Instead of a bus, you take a *vaporetto* (one *vaporetto*, some *vaporetti*), which means "little steamer." The first came from France in 1881. Since 1952 they have had diesel engines. Now there are more than a hundred, which will soon be satellite-controlled.

It's worth buying a card good for several days at one of the bigger stops. Then you have it stamped in a machine before the first trip. Children under one meter travel free. Vaporetto lines are shown on maps. You can get a special vaporetto map at the tourist office. The number 1 line is excellent. It leaves every ten minutes and makes all stops along the Grand Canal (though it says *accelerato* on it).

Sit down in front!

The numbers 41 and 42 are boats called *motoscafi*. They go around the town and out to Murano. On old maps, they are called 52 or 5. The boat from the airport has its last stop near St. Mark's Square. You buy a ticket in the arrival hall at Marco Polo. Departure once every hour. More expensive than the bus, but cheaper than a taxi boat.

How the horses came to Stockholm in 1989

The sculptor Sivert Lindblom was commissioned to decorate Blasieholm Square. The Royal Castle used to keep a stable there for its horses, so Sivert wanted to make it a horse square. By chance, he found that there were two plaster models of the Venetian horses in Sweden. So why make new ones, when the finest were already there, thought Sivert. He ordered bronze copies of the horses from Bergman's art foundry and designed their pedestals and also the square's streetlamps, fountain, and flower urns. One horse, which he calls the Old One, stands nearest to Arsenal Street. He is calm and safe and slightly bowlegged in front. The Young One, with slightly laid-back ears, stands by Stall Street and looks

Here come the horses on the truck

nervously at the Royal Castle. Two similar horses are on Rottneros in Värmland, one in Örebro and one in Östersund. All these horses are cast from two plaster models belonging to the Glyptotek in Copenhagen. The four horses on the Arc de Triomphe at the Place du Carrousel in Paris are copies of the Venetian horses, but unfortunately a French sculptor in the 1800s "improved" them.

The lion of Piraeus

(Pages 11, 34–35) In 1687 a Venetian, Francesco Morosini, stole the lion from Greece. In the harbor of Athens, Piraeus, it spouted water through its mouth into a stone bowl. The Vikings scribbled on it about 1040. Now it stands guard over the Arsenal, but the soldiers used the lion for target practice, so it is worse for wear. The Viking runes are clearer on the plaster copy in the Historical Museum in Stockholm.

Going to museums

Opening times and special exhibitions are listed in *Un Ospite di Venezia*. The Accademia is the biggest art gallery, a little tiring for children (see pp. 60–62). One of the smallest is **Scuola di San Giorgio degli Schiavoni** (pp. 72–75). It has nine paintings by Vittore Carpaccio, made between 1502 and 1507. Rather unusual opening times. Check before going to Calle dei Furlani near the canal Rio della Pietà in Castello.

Querini Stampalia is another fine smaller museum which has a library and a special garden. It's in the Castello district, behind the big church of Santa Maria Formosa. There are paintings by

The Booth of the Lion by Pietro Longhi, 1762

Still life by Hans von Essen, 1600s

Gabriel Bella and Pietro Longhi, who painted everyday subjects in the 1700s. **Museo Storico Navale**, by the dock on the far side of the Rio dell'Arsenale, is fun for those who like model boats. Everything from the Doge's famous boat *Bucintoro* to U-boats and a large shell collection.

Foreign painters in Venice

Renoir, Ruskin, Singer Sargent, Turner, Zorn, and many more. Claude Monet was there with his wife, Alice, from Sept. 30 to Dec. 7, 1908. Monet's step-great-grandson, Philippe Piguet, has written a fine book called **Monet et Venise**, with both Monet's Venice paintings and Alice's letters home to the children (Paris: Herscher, 1986).

Going shopping

Venice is abuzz with tourist shops. Many have similar dull things: small glass objects, masks, T-shirts with *Venezia* on them, and so on. The closer to St. Mark's, the more expensive. But there are also exciting shops.

Candy stores are plentiful, and they are really something. The only problem is making a choice. Our favorite, **Pasticceria Marchini,** is between two squares: San Stefano and San Maurizio.

The **record shop** across plays beautiful music, so you can hear where it is. Vivaldi is Venice's own composer, but they have plenty of others.

Paper

Marbled paper and notebooks are Venetian specialities, along with elegant pens, kaleidoscopes, and all manner of boxes. There are lots of interesting boutiques between St. Mark's and the Accademia.

Bookshops

Oh, all those beautiful books! The only drawback is that most are in Italian, including children's books, of course. But there are a good many in English and French, too.

Sansovino is the art bookshop behind the northwest corner of St. Mark's, near Bacino Orseolo.

Luciano Filippi is on Calle della Bissa in the San Marco district, and has Filippi publishers' own books on Venice and their old postcards. Time stands still; it's lovely.

Toletta is in Dorsoduro on Sacca Toletta by the Toletta Canal.

The children's bookstore, Il Librario a San Barnaba in Dorsoduro, is not easy to find. It's in an alley near Campo San Barnaba. Address: 2835 A Dorsoduro.

Suggested reading

Some guidebooks

There are many guidebooks on Venice. A few that are interesting to read both at home and in Venice are:

Venice (Everyman Guides, Alfred A. Knopf, Inc, New York, 1993), **Venice and the Veneto** (Eyewitness Travel Guides Series, 1995), **Venice** (Insight Guides, 1998), and **Exploring Venice** (Fodor's Travel Publications, 1998). These guidebooks contain many color photos, and they tell the history of Venice and describe what you can see in the city and the surrounding islands. **Rough Guide to Venice** (Viking Penguin, 1994) is a detailed, exhaustive guide. You won't see any color photographs, but you will be extremely well-informed! You will also find an excellent, up-to-date selection of hotels, restaurants, cafés.

Adult books

Jan Morris, **The World of Venice** (Alfred A. Knopf, Inc., 1993)
Jan Morris, **The Venetian Empire: A Sea Voyage** (Viking Penguin, 1990)

Some writers on Venice

Joseph Brodsky, **Watermark.** (Farrar, Straus and Giroux, 1992)
Lord Byron, letter to John Murray, February 21, 1821
(in **Byron's**

Letters and Journals (Books on
Demand, 1973)

Giacomo Casanova, **History of My
Life** (Johns Hopkins, 1997)

Johan Wolfgang Goethe, **Italian
Journey** (in **Goethe, The
Collected Works**, Volume 6
(Princeton University,
1994)

Ernest Hemingway,
**Across the River and
into the Trees** (Simon & Schuster,
1997)

Erica Jong, **Serenissima** (Houghton
Mifflin, 1987)

Thomas Mann, **Death in Venice and
Other Stories** (Bantam, 1988)

Marcel Proust, **In Search of Lost
Time** (Volume 6, Random House,
1998)

John Ruskin, **The Stones of Venice**
(Da Capo, 1985)

William Shakespeare, **The Merchant
of Venice** (Da Capo, 1985)

There are also many detective novels.
Look up "Venice" at the library and
you will see. Try Donna Leon's series,
set in Venice, which begins with
Death at La Fenice.

Finally, some dates

300 B. C.: The horses are made in
Greece?

A. D. 300: The horses are made in Rome?

A. D. 67: St. Mark killed in Alexandria

401: Alaric's Goths take northern Italy

421: Venice founded, March 25

452: Attila's Huns plunder Venice

570: Lombards take Venice

726: Venice's first Doge, Orso Ipato

828: Mark's body stolen from Alexandria
and hidden in St. Mark's Church

976: Fire in St. Mark's

1171: Venice divided into six districts

1173: First Rialto Bridge built

1203: Venice takes Constantinople

1204: The horses come to Venice

1271–95: Marco Polo goes to China

1291: Glassworks moved to Murano

1309: Doge's Palace begun

1348–49: Black Death kills half the
population of Venice

1380: Venice rules Mediterranean

1453: Turks take Constantinople

1516: Jews confined to the Ghetto in
Venice

1562: Gondolas must be black

1575: Plague in Venice

1577: Plague ends; 51,000 dead

1630: Plague returns to Venice

1718: Venice loses naval supremacy

1720: Café Florian opens

1755: Casanova imprisoned

1792: Fenice Theater opens, March 16

1797: Napoleon takes the Veneto. Last
Doge, Lodovico Manin, leaves.
Napoleon removes the horses
and gives the Veneto to Austria

1804: Napoleon becomes King of Italy

1815: Napoleon is defeated
Horses returned to Venice

1818: Lord Byron swims the Grand Canal

1836: Fenice Theater burns down

1837: Fenice is rebuilt

1846: Venice builds first railway bridge

1848: Venice rebels against Austria

1866: Venice freed from Austria,
becomes part of Italy

1885: First Biennale art exhibition
includes Monet and Renoir

1902: Campanile falls, July 4, 10 a.m.

1914: World War I breaks out

1918: World War I ends. Peace

1932: First Venice film festival

1939: World War II breaks out

1943: Mussolini takes power in Italy

1945: World War II ends
Peace once more

1966: Venice's worst flood

1979: Venice carnival reopens

1983: Groundwater pumping
banned

1996: Fenice Theater burns down,
January 29

VENICE
Venezia

CANNAREGIO

CANAL GRANDE

Railway Station
S. Lucia

S. CROCE

S. POLO

Piazzale
Roma

CANAL GRANDE

DORSODURO

Campo
S. Stefano

Accademia
Bridge

Campo
del Traghetto

Gondola Yard

Accademia
Museum

Zattere

LA GIUDECCA